Fairy Lanterns

By Tennant Redbank

Illustrated by Denise Shimabukuro, Doug Ball,
Adrienne Brown & Charles Pickens

Disney PRESS

New York

Printed and manufactured in China
First edition
1 3 5 7 9 10 8 6 4 2

Library of Congress catalog card number: 2007922741
ISBN-13: 978-1-4231-0818-4
ISBN-10: 1-4231-0818-3

Produced by becker&mayer!, Bellevue, Washington
www.beckermayer.com

VISIT WWW.DISNEYFAIRIES.COM

Far, far away, where the edge of Pixie Hollow meets the rest of Never Land, a lone sparrow man perched at the top of a tall pine tree in the dead of night. Skylar stared off into the darkness, watching and waiting.

From many meters below him, a sound reached Skylar's pointed ears. He heard the clatter of wheels on pebbles. He heard the squeak of mice.

Skylar grabbed the lantern next to him and set the wick inside on fire. He raised the lantern high. Its bright glow beamed a message across the darkness. It was time!

Some fairies didn't like being far from the Home Tree, but Tinker Bell didn't mind. She'd had adventures all over Never Land, from the pirate ship to the Mermaid Lagoon to the hideout where Peter Pan lived with the Lost Boys.

But what Tink did mind was waiting.

"Where is it?" she muttered as she paced along a narrow tree branch. Then a flash of light on the horizon caught her eye. "Skylar's lantern!" she cried. She lit her lantern and darted straight up in the air, like a rocket shot from a cannon.

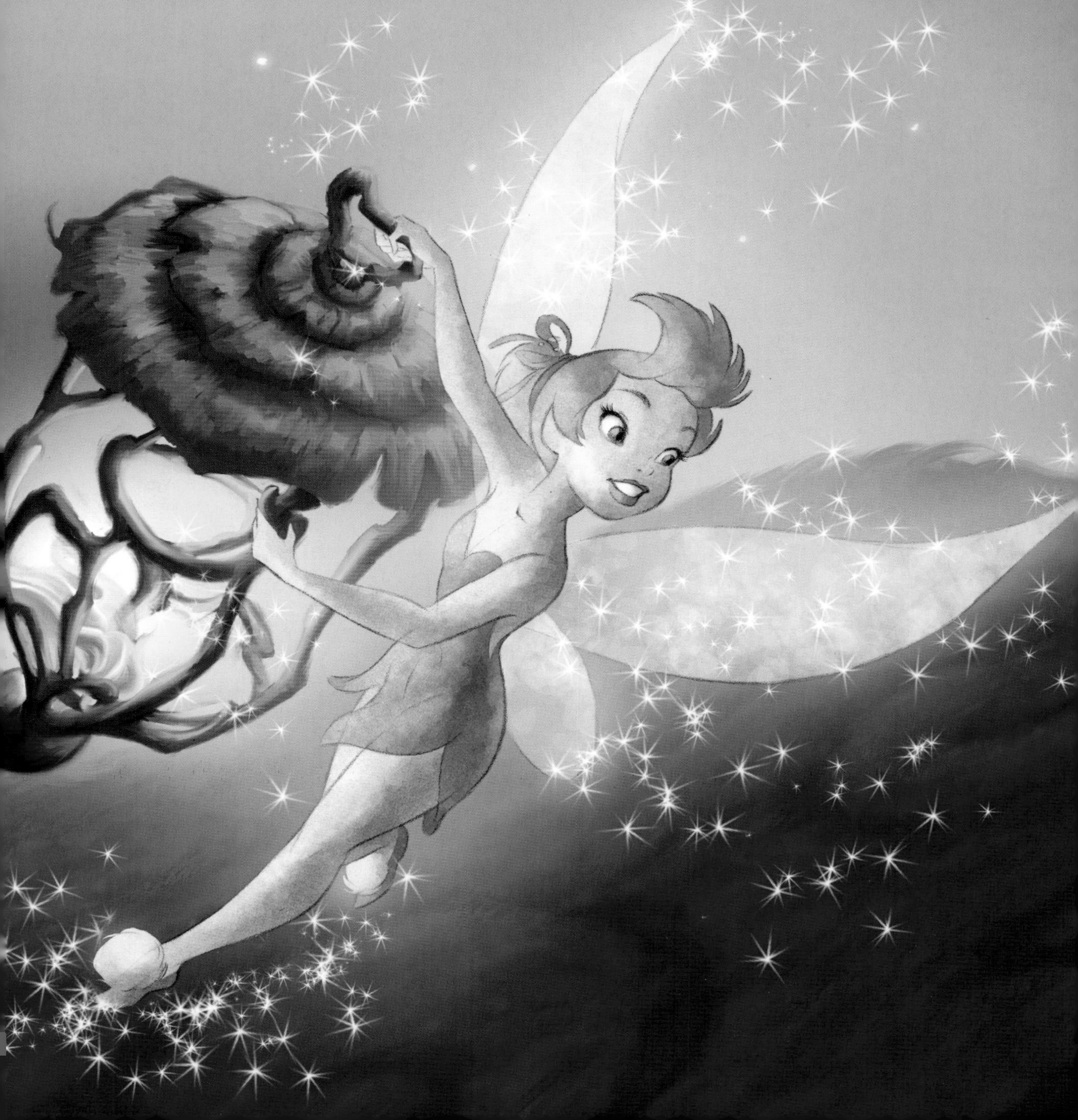

"I'm a fast-flying fairy, for pixie's sake!" Vidia complained to herself in the sour plum tree that was her home. "I could get the message there in plenty of time." But despite her grumbling, she kept a careful eye on the dark sky. And when she saw light flame through the air like a shooting star, she moved quickly to light her own lantern.

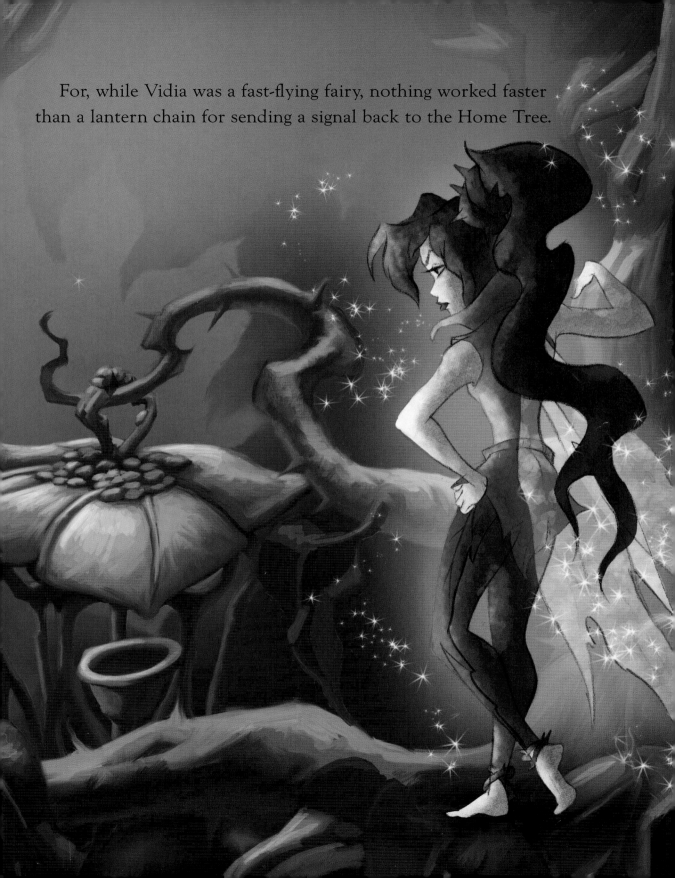

For, while Vidia was a fast-flying fairy, nothing worked faster than a lantern chain for sending a signal back to the Home Tree.

"Any luck?" Beck asked Nutley in squirrel language. Though fairies had wonderful eyesight, it wasn't as good as a squirrel's. But Nutley hadn't spotted anything, either.

Beck leaned against Nutley. He wrapped his tail around her and offered her part of a hazelnut.

Then, clear as day, a burst of light came from the direction of the sour plum tree. Nutley and Beck jumped up. In an instant, Beck's lantern was lit and Nutley had carried it to the top of a tree where everyone could see it.

Fira nervously nibbled on her fingernails and searched the sky. Night after night and day after day, the fairies had kept a lookout. When would they get the sign?

Off in the distance, a dot of light appeared. Fira yelled, "Hurry, Flicker!"

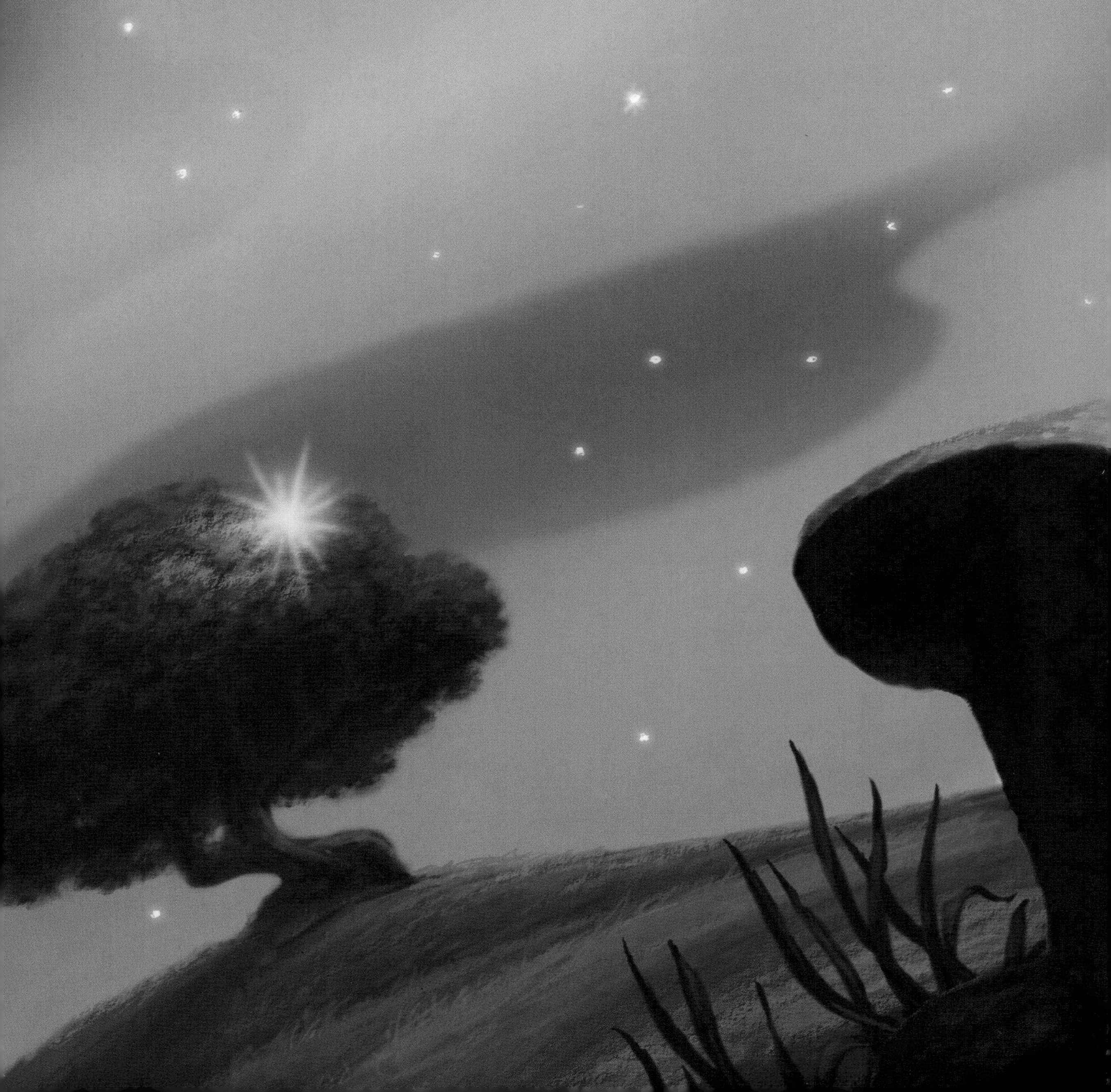

Flicker the firefly crawled into the lantern and lit it up as brightly as any flame. Just to be sure, Fira turned up her own glow several notches. It was a signal no one could miss!

"I don't mind waiting," Rani told Brother Dove, "as long as I'm in a place like this."

Rani loved listening to Havendish Stream as it rushed over the rocks. But the second she saw Fira's glow, her thoughts of water were replaced by thoughts of light.

"Did you see it, Brother Dove? It's so bright!" Rani cried. She jumped onto Brother Dove's back, and, taking flight, they added their light to the chain of lanterns that stretched across Pixie Hollow.

Lily was so busy admiring her garden, she almost missed Rani's signal. "Look at the way the sunflowers close their blooms so tightly," she said. "And the moonflowers open up to catch the moonbeams!" She dropped to her knees to admire the patch of night bloomers, her lantern forgotten next to her. But a twinkle at the corner of her eye called her back to the job at hand.

"Oh! That's the signal!" she cried. Lily lit the lantern and held it high. "I hope they can see it back at the Home Tree," she said.

Dulcie had no problem spotting Lily's light from the window of the Home Tree kitchen. "It's time! It's time!" she yelled to the other kitchen fairies. "We have to hurry. Finish everything and then get over to the courtyard right away! And someone send a messenger to wake all the other fairies!"

The fairies sprang into action. "Let's hope it's not a false alarm," Dulcie added under her breath.

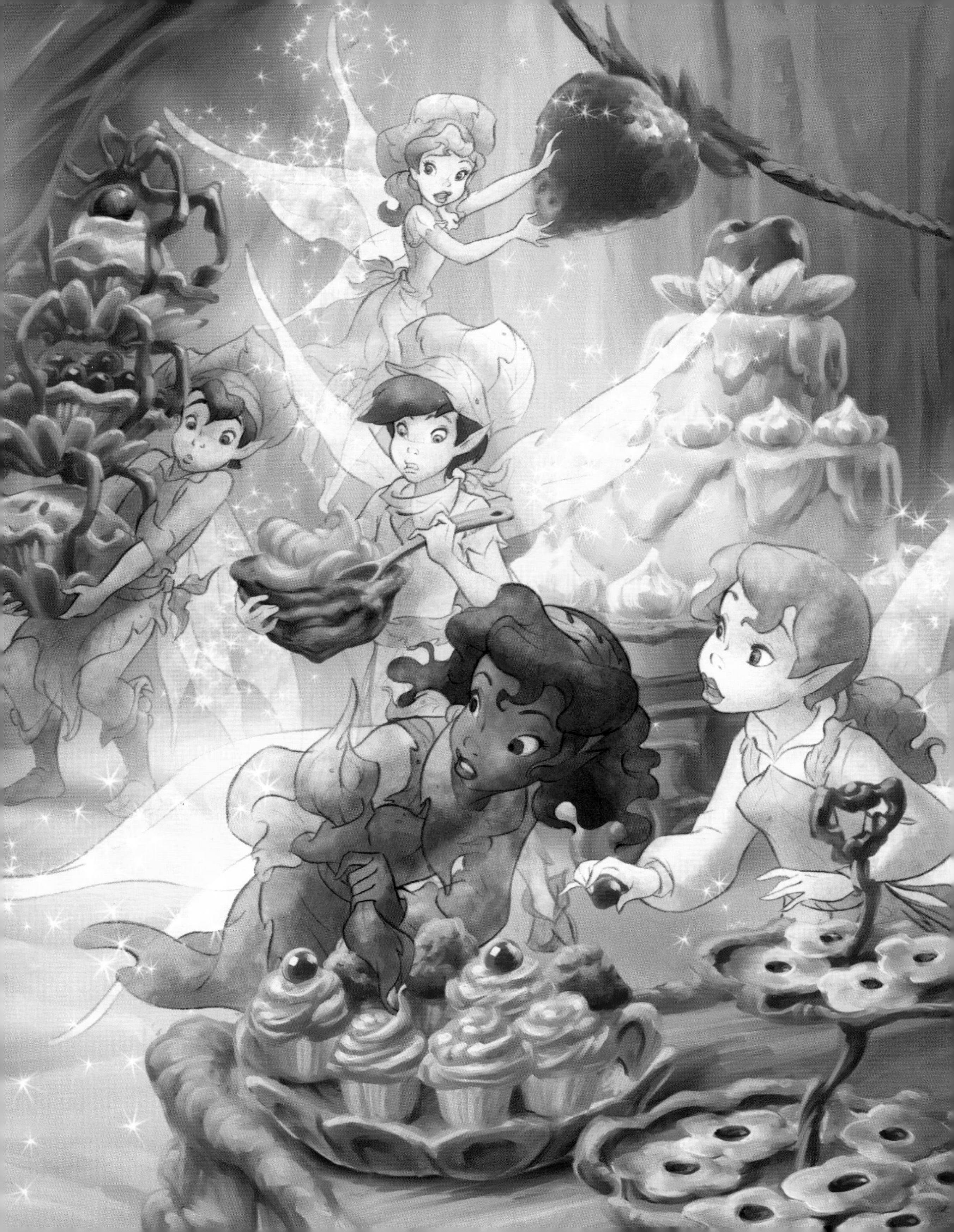

All the fairies and sparrow men gathered in the Home Tree courtyard. The lantern chain had worked so well, Lily, Beck, Fira, Rani, Vidia, and Tink had made it back in plenty of time. Even Skylar, who had been furthest away, was nearly home.

The courtyard hummed with suspense.
"I hear them coming!" Tink whispered. "Be quiet, everyone!"
"Put out your lights," Fira told the fireflies.
The courtyard was completely still, dark, and silent.

Two gray mice pulled a snail-shell carriage up to the Home Tree. Through the carriage window, Queen Clarion looked out at the dark courtyard. "It's good to be home," she said. She had traveled all the way to Torth Mountain to make sure the dragon Kyto was still securely locked in his cage. Although Clarion loved her job as fairy queen, she didn't like it when her duties took her away from Pixie Hollow for so long.

"I guess I'll have to wait until morning to see everyone," she added with a sigh.

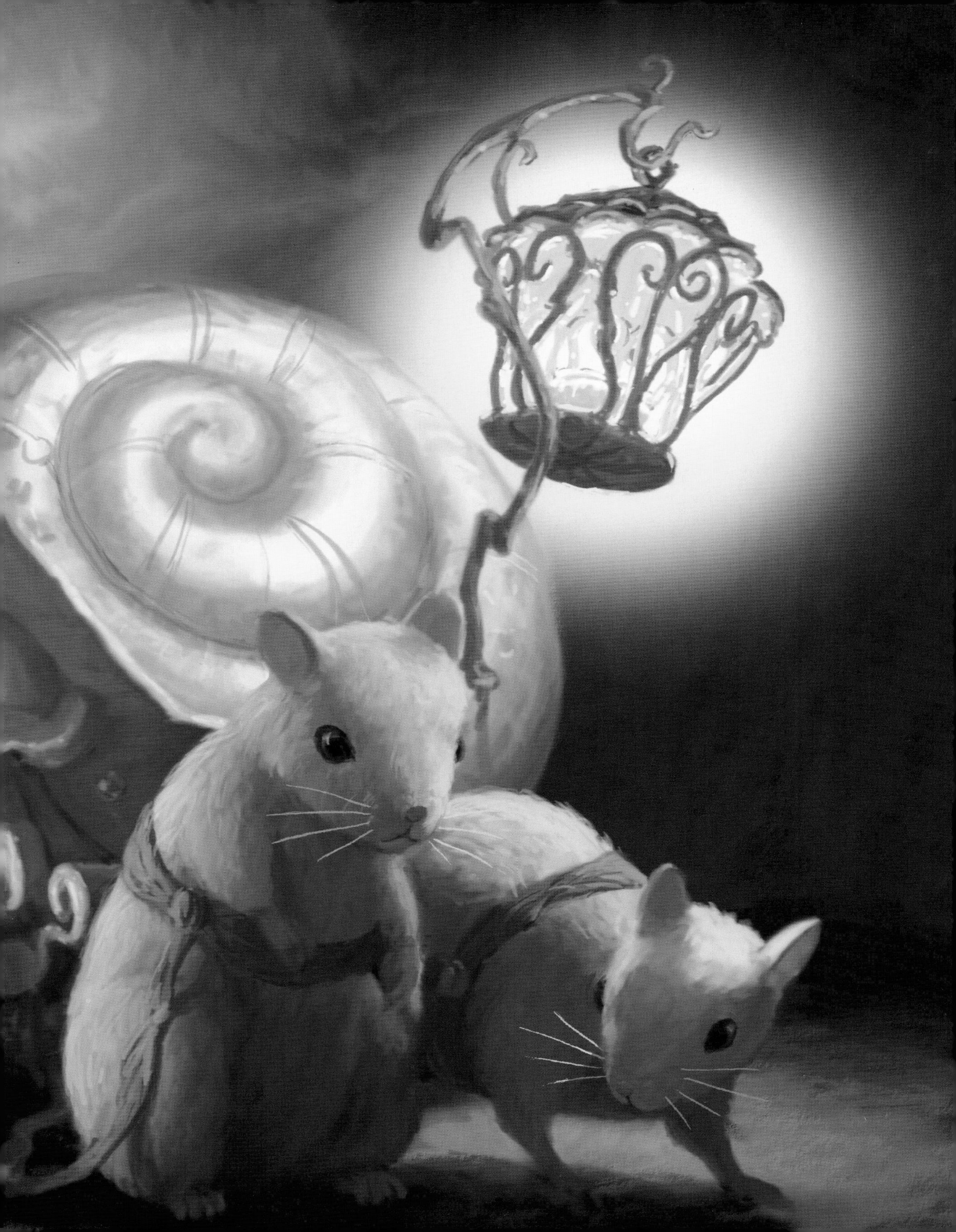

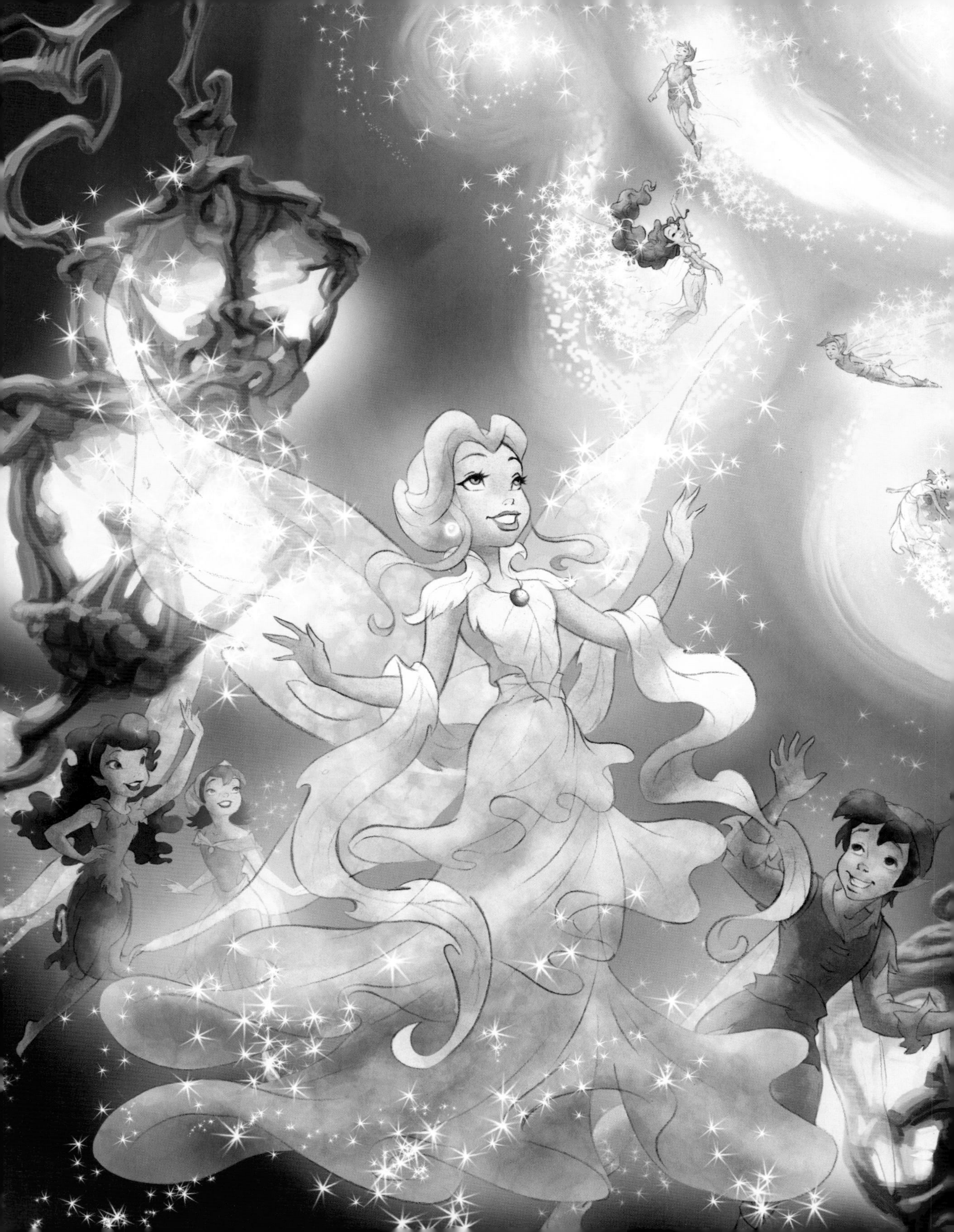

Queen Clarion stepped down from the carriage and turned toward the Home Tree. At that instant, a blaze of light lit up the courtyard, dazzling her eyes. On every side of her stood smiling fairies and sparrow men with colorful lanterns. Light-talent fairies sent sparks shooting into the sky like fireworks. "Welcome home, Queen Clarion!" they all cried.

Everyone was so happy to see Queen Clarion that they didn't want to go to sleep. The festive event went on late into the night. Music talents played songs; storytelling fairies told tall tales; everyone danced a fairy-circle dance; and the moon shone down on the happy Never fairy realm.